3 1783 00505 0723

W9-BMY-358

Fox River Valley PLD
555 Barrington Ave., Dundee, IL 60118
www.frvpld.info
Renew online or call 847-590-8706

written and illustrated by
Elisabeth Zuniga

A Friend for Bo

Bo

Random House 🏠 New York

Visit us on the Web!
randomhousekids.com

Educators and librarians, for a variety of teaching tools, visit us at
RHTeachersLibrarians.com

Library of Congress Cataloging-in-Publication Data
Zuniga, Elisabeth, author, illustrator.
A friend for Bo / by Elisabeth Zuniga. — First edition.
pages cm.
Summary: "Bo is lonely. So he sets out to find a new friend. And that new friend
just happens to be . . . an egg!" —Provided by publisher.
ISBN 978-0-553-50998-4 (trade) — ISBN 978-0-553-50999-1 (lib. bdg.) —
ISBN 978-0-553-51000-3 (ebook)
[1. Friendship—Fiction. 2. Eggs—Fiction.] I. Title.
PZ7.1.Z86 Fr 2016 [E]—dc23 2014039344

MANUFACTURED IN CHINA

10 9 8 7 6 5 4 3 2 1
First Edition

*For Mummy and Pop—my best friends ever. And for Katheryne,
Carolyne, Amie, Ashleigh, Caitlyn, David, Jemmy, AbbeyRose, Bonnie,
Land, and Truly—my first playmates and forever friends.*

—E.Z.

It was a perfect day for playing.
Except for one thing—
Bo had no one to play *with*.
So he set out to find a friend.

"What's this?" Bo asked.

"Hello?"

"Why, hello!"

"You seem rather shy,"
Bo said. "That's okay.
I like shy."
Bo named his new
friend Rollie.

Bo took Rollie home.

"Let's play dress-up,"
suggested Bo.

But Rollie didn't reply.

"Or maybe you'd like
to read a story?"

But Rollie couldn't see
the pictures!

So Bo helped him out.

Now Rollie smiled.

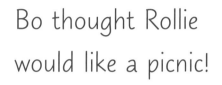

Bo thought Rollie
would like a picnic!

Along the way, Bo saw three butterflies.
"Look!" Bo said to Rollie. "Butterflies!"

But Rollie didn't look.

"Surprise!" said Bo.
"We're going sailing!"
But Rollie didn't say anything.

"Here, have a cookie," Bo said.

But Rollie didn't take one.
And when the little boat rocked,
Rollie dove right into the picnic basket!

"Oh no!
You smashed
the cookies!"

Bo was so sad.
But Rollie just smiled.

"I think we should go now," Bo said.

But Rollie didn't want to leave.

So Bo had to help him
out of the boat. . . .

"Well, I hope *you* had a good time today," said Bo.

When they got home, Bo
was ready to call it a day.
So was Rollie.

"Won't you please make
room for me?" asked Bo.
But Rollie didn't budge.

Poor Bo curled up on the rug
and fell fast asleep—until . . .

"Oh, Rollie, what's the matter?"
Bo asked.
Then he heard a loud . . .

"What a lovely surprise!"

Peep.

Peep.

Bo knew EXACTLY what to do
with a little duckling . . .

PLAY!

And the little duckling
loved to play.

Now Bo has two friends!
But Rollie still doesn't talk much.